This book belongs to...

_____

© Illus. Dr. Seuss 1957

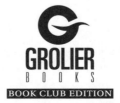

GROLIER
B O O K S
BOOK CLUB EDITION

Frogs
in
Clogs

by
Sheila
White
Samton

A Bright & Early Book
From BEGINNER BOOKS
A Division of Random House, Inc.

Random House 🏠 New York

For Pat Stiles

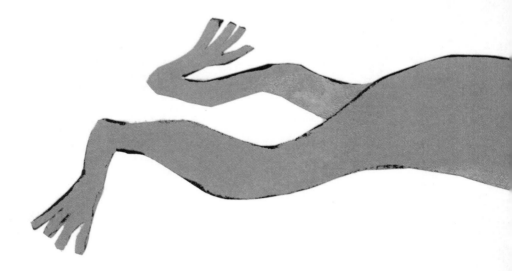

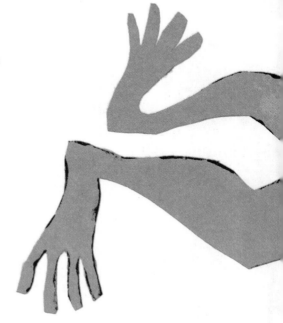

Originally published by Crown Publishers, Inc., in 1995

Published by special arrangement
with Random House Children's Books,
a division of Random House, Inc.

Grolier Books is a division of Grolier Enterprises, Inc.

Library of Congress Cataloging-in-Publication Data
Samton, Sheila White.
Frogs in clogs / written and illustrated by Sheila White Samton. — 1st ed.
p. cm.
Summary: Frogs in clogs befriend pigs in wigs and together
they outwit the greedy bugs on rugs.
[1. Animals—Fiction. 2. Stories in rhyme.] I.Title.
PZ8.3.S213Fr   1995
[E]—dc20   94-16391

ISBN 0-517-59874-4 (trade)
0-517-59875-2 (lib. bdg.)

BRIGHT & EARLY BOOKS is a registered trademark of Random House, Inc.

*The illustrations in this book are collages of
avrylic paint on rice paper.
The text is set in Leawood Book.*

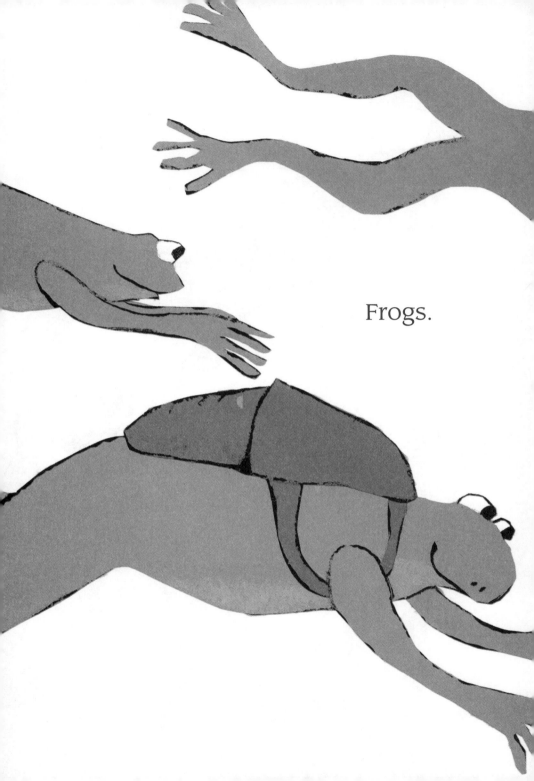

Frogs.

Bog.

Frogs in the bog.

Boggy frogs.
Soggy frogs.

Frogs in clogs!

Pigs.

Figs.

Pigs in the figs.

Piggy pigs. Figgy pigs.

Pigs in wigs!

Pigs in wigs jig into the bog.

Frogs joggle pigs!
Pigs jiggle frogs!

Would you like to share our figs?

Would you like to wear our clogs?

Frogs and pigs
wiggle-woggle
in the bog!

Bugs on rugs,
wearing goggles
in a fog!

Would you like to share our figs?

Bugs want *all* the figs, clogs, wigs!

BIG STRUGGLE IN THE BOG!

Bugs lug pigs to rugs in fog!

Fig on a log?
Fig on a wig?

Follow the figs!
Find our pigs!

Good-bye, bugs.
Big frog hugs!